The Mystery
of the
Dead Sea Scrolls

Hagit Allon and Lena Zehavi

Illustrated by Yossi Abolafia

THE JEWISH PUBLICATION SOCIETY

Philadelphia 5764•2003

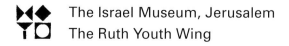

The Israel Museum, Jerusalem
The Ruth Youth Wing

This publication was made possible by the generous support of
Ernst and Thilde Fraenkel, London

Published and distributed (except in Israel) by The Jewish Publication
Society, 2100 Arch Street, Philadelphia, PA 19103

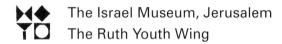

The Israel Museum, Jerusalem
The Ruth Youth Wing

The Mystery of the Dead Sea Scrolls

Hagit Allon and Lena Zehavi
Illustrated by Yossi Abolafia

Curator-in-charge: Nurit Shilo-Cohen
Production coordinator: Liora Vogelman

Graphic design: Studio Rami & Jacki / Gadi Gershon
Design consultant: Nirit Zur
Translation: Malka Jagendorf, Kathy Beller
Copy editing: Anna Barber
For photo credits and captions, see p. 60
Printed and bound in China

ISBN 965 278 276 9

Chapter 1 | I Have an Assignment to Do

First let me tell you who I am. My name is Daniel. I live in Jerusalem and I'm eleven. I'm skinny, not very tall, and I wear glasses. Sometimes kids in my class laugh at me and call me "Professor." But in the 60-meter race, I am the fastest in my class and this gives me credit with the other kids.

Ever since I was little I've liked nature and detective stories. Sometimes when I have nothing to do, I imagine how it would feel to be a detective, and I go out and practice in the neighborhood with my little brother, Jonathan, who is six.

I watch our neighbor, Judith, when she stops to feed the cats on her way to the grocery store. I follow my teacher, Dorit, as she leaves school. At the same time, I try to note the license numbers of the cars that pass by. You never know – something could happen and I'd be the first to report it to the police!

I was beginning to give up, because in spite of all my watching, nothing was happening. At least not until the day Dorit handed out projects and I was assigned a report on the Dead Sea Scrolls. She said it was a good idea for me to visit the Shrine of the Book at the Israel Museum, and so the next day I found myself riding to the Museum to check out these scrolls.

The bus was pretty full. There were shoppers coming home from the market, school kids, and two tourists with backpacks. But what made me really curious was an oldish man in dark glasses seated in front of me, holding a folded newspaper in a foreign language. He looked like spies I had seen in movies or read about in books. I decided to keep an eye on him, and before I knew it we had reached the bus stop near the Museum and the man in the dark glasses stood up to get off the bus just like me. He walked slowly towards the Museum entrance, going through the glass doors – with me close behind him – and headed exactly where I was going: the Shrine of the Book.

It was only the beginning of the summer, but it was a hot, dry day. The fountain splashing over the Shrine of the Book cooled the air. Now the man sat on the railing near the dome, opposite the black wall. He seemed to be waiting for someone. I waited, too, but nothing happened.

"How long can a person stare at a black wall and a white dome?" I wondered.

A sign with an arrow pointed to the entrance. I skipped down the stairs and jogged into the building.

"Young man, no running, please. This is not a soccer field," said the guard at the entrance. He was short, with a stiff moustache and a starchy uniform. He looked very serious. Not to mention the pistol strapped to his side. I felt uneasy and he looked annoyed.

Inside it was cool and dark. At first I couldn't see anything. When I got used to the dim light, I saw that this room was not like any of the other galleries in the Museum. Exactly opposite me, there was a black wall, similar to the one I had seen outside. In the middle of the wall there was an opening.

Puzzled, I asked the guard, "Excuse me, is this where the Dead Sea Scrolls are kept?"

Still looking stern, the guard replied: "Young man, are you here by yourself? Didn't I already tell you that this is no place for playing around; what are you doing here?"

"I have to write a project on the Dead Sea Scrolls," I answered nervously.

"The scrolls are down that way at the end of the corridor under the dome," said the guard, "but remember they are the Museum's most precious treasure. So be as quiet and respectful as you can."

If he stands here every day, he must know a lot more about the scrolls than me, I thought – maybe I could learn something from him.

"What do you mean the most precious treasure?" I asked scornfully. "They're just ordinary scrolls, they're not even made of gold."

"Just ordinary scrolls?" said the guard. "Why, they are the most important treasure that the Jewish people have, more precious than any gold treasure. Children today have no respect for anything!" he

muttered under his cap.

"Tell me," he asked, "do you learn Bible in school?"

"Sure," I answered expecting a lecture right there and then.

"Well, the scrolls that are here are genuine books of the Bible – very old Bibles – in fact, 2,000 years old. They were copied down by Jews who lived here, in Israel, when the Temple was still standing," explained the guard.

"So they're really real?" I asked him.

"Of course," said the guard, "and more than that. They were written in ink on parchment made from animal skins."

I remembered that in our last science class, we had talked about the environment and the teacher had told us that things made from animals and plants spoil quickly. I wanted to show the guard that I also knew a thing or two.

"Skin rots and crumbles," I said.

"That's right," said the guard, "but these scrolls were found in a cave in the Judean desert. The darkness in the cave and the dryness of the climate were perfect for preserving the parchment, and so the scrolls were saved."

"But what is written on them?" I asked.

"In the caves, fragments from all the books of the Bible were found, from Genesis to Chronicles, meaning the first to the last, except for the books of Nehemiah and Esther. Some of the books were found in more than one copy," said the guard.

"Are all the scrolls here?" I asked.

"No," answered the guard, "only the most beautiful and important ones are on display here. And now I have work to do. Go inside, but quietly."

I thanked the guard and walked through the dark corridor into

the dome. It was a circular room, and all along the wall there were long, narrow glass cases with scrolls inside. I tried to read them, but it was hard to make out the letters.

I saw that each showcase had a red button beside it. I was a bit uncomfortable and I wasn't sure whether I was allowed to press the buttons. Eventually, I pressed one and a light came on. At one end of the showcase were strange little machines. I remembered what the guard had said about the darkness in the cave, and I thought to myself that this must be special equipment that protects the scrolls.

Inside the showcase stretched a long, brown scroll with edges that looked like they had been burnt. Up close I saw that the scroll was made of pieces of parchment sewn together. The writing was very clear. I tried to sketch the writing in the notebook I had brought with me, but the light in the showcase kept switching off. I switched it on again and again, until I had finished my sketch. The label next to the showcase said this was the "Community Rule" scroll. That meant nothing to me.

I decided to check in the Museum Library. There, I thought, I was sure to find something about the

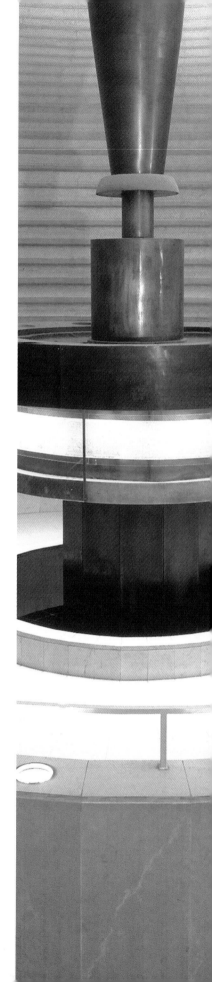

scrolls. The librarian, a tall and very enthusiastic woman, smiled at me. She immediately pointed me in the direction of the Dead Sea Scroll section. There were loads of books there, but most of them were in hard English and seemed very complicated. This was too much.

I looked at my watch and I saw that I had to get home. Whatever there was to find at the Museum would have to wait for tomorrow or maybe the next day.

Chapter 2 | Making Friends with the Man on the Bus

I returned to the Museum a few days later. This time, the guard remembered me and let me right in. I entered, and I discovered to my surprise that the man in dark glasses from the bus was sitting reading sheets of paper spread out on his lap. I sat down nearby, opened my notebook, and pretended to write while watching him out of the corner of my eye.

There was something interesting but definitely strange about him. In the meantime, a group of kibbutzniks entered with a guide. I jumped up and joined them. I wanted to hear what the guide was saying.

"My friends," began the guide, "the story of the scrolls is a fascinating one. The scrolls were discovered by chance, some fifty years ago, by a little Bedouin shepherd boy from the Tamra tribe, Muhammad al-Zeeb, which means 'wolf.'"

"Wow," I thought to myself, "what a great name!"

"The boy," the guide told his audience, "was tending his goats in Qumran on the shores of the Dead Sea, when he realized that one of the goats was missing. Muhammad searched for the goat and came to a cave on a cliffside. He threw a stone into the cave's opening and heard the sound of pottery breaking. Out of curiosity, he climbed into the cave and

saw large jars inside, some of them broken. Terrified, he ran out. The next day, he returned to the cave with some friends. The boys discovered seven complete scrolls and around twenty small fragments."

"Boy," I thought, "why wasn't I a Bedouin shepherd? Who knows what I might have found in the desert?"

I noticed that the man sitting near me was also listening, although he did not seem to be happy about what he heard.

The guide continued: "The Bedouins kept the scrolls for a few weeks. They used the jars for water, and planned to make sandals from the sheepskin scrolls. In the end, they decided to bring the scrolls to a Christian shoemaker named Kando in Bethlehem, who was also an antiquities merchant. Thank goodness, the shoemaker could read, so he realized that something very important had come his way. He immediately contacted a church leader in Jerusalem and told him about the discovery, suggesting that he meet with the Bedouins.

"The church leader agreed but forgot to tell the monastery guard that he should expect the Bedouins. When the guard saw three shabby, unshaven men asking to be admitted, he refused to open the gate and sent them away. The Bedouins were deeply offended, and one of them sold his share, three scrolls, to an Armenian antiquities dealer. Kando the shoemaker bought the four remaining scrolls.

"The Armenian dealer sold his three scrolls to Professor Eliezer Sukenik of the Hebrew University, and later Professor Yigael Yadin bought the other four. Today all of them are here, in the Shrine of the Book."

The guide had finished the story, and he continued on with his group of kibbutzniks.

I stayed sitting in my place. The story sounded like it had been made up. The scrolls had been found completely by chance! Out of the corner of my eye I saw the man from the bus. He waved his hand, shifted into a more comfortable position, and signaled me to come over.

"Since you are already writing," he said, "you ought to know the whole story. It's not all that simple."

I was a bit nervous, but felt better when I saw the guard nearby, as well as some other tourists viewing the exhibits. "What could happen?" I asked myself, and moved closer to the man.

"On Saturday, November 29, 1947, Professor Sukenik was given three scrolls and two jars to examine. These were the days before the establishment of the State of Israel, and the roads were dangerous. Professor Sukenik was the head of the Archaeology Department at the Hebrew University. He risked his life traveling to Bethlehem to get the scrolls. At night, when he inspected the scrolls in his room, he heard the broadcast from the United Nations in New York, where the nations voted to establish the State of Israel. Sukenik was overwhelmed, filled with excitement by this amazing coincidence. It seemed as if the scrolls had waited in those caves for 2,000 years from the destruction of the Temple to the establishment of a new Jewish state. The professor decided to buy the three scrolls. The very next day, the War of Independence broke out and Sukenik did not manage to acquire the four remaining scrolls. They traveled on a long journey and ended up in a bank vault in New York.

"Sukenik had a son called Yigael Yadin, who was the second Commander-in-Chief of the new State of Israel. When he left the

army, he returned to his studies and also became a professor of archaeology. In 1954, a year after his father died, Yigael Yadin flew to America on a lecture tour.

"One day the phone rang in Yadin's hotel room. The caller identified himself as a journalist. He explained to the professor that he had seen an advertisement in a newspaper offering four ancient scrolls for sale. Yadin immediately contacted the Prime Minister of Israel at the time, David Ben-Gurion, and also Teddy Kollek – yes, yes, the same Teddy Kollek who was the mayor of Jerusalem for twenty-five years; in those days he was Ben-Gurion's advisor. With the help of a donation from an American Jewish businessman, Samuel Gottesman, the State of Israel bought the scrolls for the sum of $250,000. Samuel Gottesman also provided the money to build a home for the scrolls – the building we're sitting in right now – which was given the name 'the Shrine of the Book.'"

"How do you know all this?" I asked.

"My name is Solomon Even-Chen, and I am a journalist," he said. "During the War of Independence, I was badly wounded and while I was recovering, I took my first steps as a reporter. All the important journalists were busy writing about the war and the struggle for independence, and it was left to me to write about Professor Sukenik and the scrolls. Ever since then I have had the "scroll" bug and I follow every new turn of events in the story of the scrolls. It's amazing how things that happened over two thousand years ago continue to astound the world of today. There is so much more that we don't know about this story than what we do know, so I try to publish any new information that comes up."

I was beginning to see the importance of the Dead Sea Scrolls, but I still didn't understand what the mystery was. Over fifty years had passed since they were discovered – what could still be unclear?

I told Solomon that I, too, was researching the scrolls and I added that I was getting a little confused. A look of satisfaction appeared on his face.

"What is your name?" he asked.

"Daniel," I answered.

"Well, Daniel," he said. "I think I can help you." He led me out of the Shrine, crossed the yard, and entered an office surrounded by glass walls.

In a side room full of bookshelves sat a big, broad man. He was speaking on the telephone. When he saw us, he ended the conversation, hung up, and turned to us with a smile.

"Solomon, aren't you fed up yet?" he asked my new friend.

"You know very well there's no cure when you catch the scroll bug," Solomon answered. "But now, I want to introduce you to Daniel. He also wants to write about the scrolls."

The big man got up from his chair and shook my hand warmly.

Chapter 3 | I Meet the Curator of the Shrine of the Book

"Daniel, meet the Curator of the Shrine of the Book," said Solomon. "He's in charge of all the treasures here, and he can help you more than anyone else."

Solomon left us and went on his way. And I sat tongue-tied opposite this important man.

"Well, young man, how can I help you?"

"I would like to know who wrote the scrolls, and what they wrote in them," I said. "I'm sorry to bother you, but there were so many books about them in the library, I didn't know where to begin."

"Many books written about the scrolls are too detailed and difficult to use," said the curator. "I'll try to clear things up for you."

Immediately I took out my notebook, ready and waiting to write down every word he said.

"More than two thousand years ago, at the time of the Second Temple, there were three groups of Jews living in the Land of Israel," the curator began. "There were the Sadducees – high-class and wealthy priests – and the Pharisees who represented most of the people and who were our ancestors. They were the ones who interpreted the Bible. The third group were the Essenes, who some scholars think were the

ones who wrote the scrolls."

"But what did they do in the desert?" I asked. "There is nothing in the desert."

"Good, Daniel," said the curator. "Well, the Essenes were a group that decided to leave everyday life behind and try a new existence, which they thought would be more perfect. They believed that God had chosen them from birth. They were stubborn people who created a whole system of strict laws and rules. Some of the scrolls describe in great detail how the Essenes lived in Qumran."

"Qumran?" I asked. "That sounds like a very old word."

The curator explained, "Qumran is the Arabic name for a place on the shores of the Dead Sea, where the Essenes established a settlement. That's where they lived, and that's where the caves are that hid the scrolls."

"But who wrote the scrolls?" I asked.

"The Essenes themselves," said the curator. "A few types of scrolls were found in those caves. One of them is called the 'Community Rule,' and it tells all about the Essenes' life and customs. Today the 'community' is known as the Judean Desert sect, a group of people who lived in the Judean Desert, isolating themselves far away from the cities and towns. Whoever joined the sect had to live just like the others, the way people used to live on a kibbutz. When you joined the Essenes everything you owned became the property of the sect. 'And the rich use no more than the poor who have nothing,' is how they put it.

"Members of the sect were put in charge of the joint property, from which they gave charity to the poor. Anyone interested in joining the sect had to pass a series of tests before being accepted as a full member. The Judean Desert sect had a fixed daily routine. These men left their families, to live in the desert. They prayed together and ate together, always observing personal hygiene and strict laws of purity. It seems that they believed that living with women made it harder to observe the rules of ritual purity. They observed the Sabbath and all the commandments more strictly than other Jews. They even had their own separate calendar."

"Finally I understand!" I said, jumping up from my chair. "A few days ago when I was here I saw that scroll. The name 'Community Rule' seemed so strange to me. Wait," I remembered, "there was another scroll, too, something about light and dark."

"You saw the scroll about the war between the Sons of Light and the Sons of Darkness," said the curator. "The Essenes thought the world was divided between good people and evil people. They were the good people, and the rest of the world was bad. The members of the Judean Desert sect were waiting for the Messiah, but they believed that first there would be a terrible war. They prepared for it, in the desert, in the shade of the date palms, far from other people and other settlements. The scroll of the War between the Sons of Light and the Sons of Darkness describes the war that was to come."

"Was everyone expected to fight in that war?" I asked.

"There were laws about that, too. Everybody had a task. Youngsters were expected to guard the camp while the grown-up men went out to battle," said the curator.

"Why just the grown-ups?" I asked.

"To win a war demands not just military strength, but also wisdom and maturity. That comes with age."

"What sort of weapons did they have?"

"Mostly prayers and trumpets, but also real weapons, which unfortunately we have never found."

"What else was found at Qumran?" I asked.

"A variety of everyday objects."

"Today, is there still a Judean Desert sect?"

"No," replied the curator, "the Essenes disappeared from history after the Jews' valiant but hopeless war against the Romans. When the Sons of Darkness won the war, the Essenes were terribly shaken. Many

of them died in battle, and those who remained disbanded and scattered."

The curator glanced at his watch. It was nearly closing time in the Museum.

"I hope I have helped you," he said, walking with me to the door.

I thanked him for his help and ran to the bus stop.

On the way home, I thought about the members of the sect. In my mind I pictured them living in the desert, praying and preparing for their terrible war. Why hadn't a movie been made about them?

Chapter 4 | Going to Qumran and Meeting Yigal the Archaeologist

That evening at supper, I couldn't keep quiet. I started nagging.

"Dad, what are we doing this weekend?"

"No real plans," said my father.

"I have an idea for a great outing."

"What mountain do you want us to climb and what river do you want us to cross this time?" asked Mom.

"The Judean Desert," I answered.

"In this heat?" Mom asked. She looked tired at the very thought of it.

"We could set out early in the morning," I said.

"Getting us out of bed again at the crack of dawn, on the day that we can sleep late?" Dad smiled.

"Just this once," I begged.

"This is no time for trips to the desert," said Mom in a voice that didn't leave much room for argument.

I changed my tactics. I told them about my visit to the Shrine of the Book, and how I had met the journalist and the curator. When I finished my story, Mom and Dad sat silently. It seemed to me that they were impressed. At the end, Dad said: "Well, we still have a few days. We'll think about it and see what the weather will be like on Saturday."

I didn't say another word on the subject until Friday, and to tell you the truth, it wasn't easy.

On Friday, after supper, when I was about to burst, Dad said to us in a decisive voice: "Okay, kids, go to bed now so we can make an early start tomorrow morning. Yes, yes, Daniel, we're going to the Judean Desert."

Jonathan and I rushed to our room to prepare our backpacks. I took binoculars for bird watching, a magnifying glass (a must for every outing), a penknife, plastic bags and small plastic boxes to put any evidence or artifacts we might find, a roll of scotchtape for sealing, and a compass. And of course, a map, pencil, and notebook.

I climbed into bed, but I couldn't fall asleep. I thought about the members of the sect living in the desert, and about the Bedouin boy and his goats.

When I woke up it was morning, and before I knew it we were on our way. Driving along we passed a Bedouin camp, with tents and shepherds tending sheep and goats in the hills on both sides of the road. We passed Ma'ale Adumin, and as we turned towards Jericho and approached the Dead Sea, the road became straighter and the mountains seemed to disappear.

As we drove south towards Qumran the view out of our windows widened. On our left was the sparkling Dead Sea with the mountains of Moab behind it. On the right were the barren mountains of the Judean desert.

"Wow," said Mom, "the view is incredible. It feels like we are driving into biblical times."

Nobody said anything. Sometimes Mom comes out with these enthusiastic insights that leave us all slightly stunned. It may have something to do with her job – as a psychologist, she has some weird explanation for everything.

Shortly after, we reached Qumran. The parking lot was empty, apart from two cars and a jeep.

"Look, there's hardly anyone here," Mom said, "everyone is still asleep."

"But at least it's nice and cool," said Dad.

At the foot of the mountains stood the crumbling remains of houses spread out over a large area. It was clear that these houses had no ceilings and their walls were low. We saw only the floors and the remains of walls.

Suddenly, from a ditch below, a young man with curly hair and wearing shorts appeared. He was very tanned and it seemed as if he spent a lot of time outside. A small hammer peeped out of his pocket, but his eyes were hidden behind sunglasses. He seemed to be signaling us with his hands, and then to my surprise Dad seemed to be signaling back. They ran towards each other and hugged like old friends.

"Yigal, what are you doing here?" Dad asked.

"We're preparing an archaeological excavation, and I came to have a look around by myself, before the work starts.

"And what are you doing here?"

"Our Daniel seems to have been bitten by the archaeology bug.

He's doing a project on the Dead Sea Scrolls and he's dragged us all down here," explained Dad. "Daniel's even done some research at the Israel Museum.

"Everyone," said Dad, looking at Mom, Jonathan, and me, "this is Yigal, an archaeologist and a friend of mine from my army service."

"An archaeologist!" I said. "How perfect!"

"Get ready for some cross-examination," Mom warned Yigal.

"Gladly," answered Yigal, leading the way. My little brother trailed behind. He hates ancient stuff and also hates the sun. It was clear that he was already suffering.

"The caves you see all around you are the same caves that the members of the Judean Desert sect lived in. So far 35 caves have been found, and some of them show signs that they were inhabited. The Essenes also lived in huts and tents, and in our excavations we found tent posts. It appears that about 200 people lived in Qumran – all men."

"Where did their wives live?" asked Mom.

"Not with their husbands," answered Yigal. "These men chose to leave their families and live alone in the desert."

"Mom," I interrupted, "I told you that the curator at the Museum told me that the Essenes emphasized purity – probably they thought living with women wasn't pure."

My mother looked most dissatisfied and muttered something about male chauvinism.

"What did they live on?" asked Dad.

"They grew date palms (and we really did find dried dates in the area) and planted crops that were irrigated by spring water."

"In this desert?" Dad asked.

"If you know the desert you can do a lot with it," said Yigal, "and the Essenes knew the desert very well."

"Like the Bedouins!" Jonathan piped up.

"You're right, Jonathan, but the Essenes knew it even better," Yigal said enthusiastically. He continued, "This room in front of us was the writing room. Here we found inkwells and scribes' tables, which are now in the Rockefeller Museum in Jerusalem. The members of the sect wrote all the scrolls that are now in the Shrine of the Book and many more. Altogether around 800 scroll fragments were found, 200 of them containing biblical texts.

"Now let's have a look at these pools which used to hold fresh water," said Yigal. "The men immersed themselves in these long, narrow pools in order to be purified. They walked down the steps into the pools. In between the pools, there was a dining room where the members ate and prayed together."

"Exactly the same as in the kibbutz," Mom said.

"They shared everything, and rather than minding being squashed together in the dining room, they seemed to have enjoyed it."

We passed another large pool, and saw a workshop where the potter made all the dishes and cooking pots from clay.

NORTH
CLOISTER

It was nearly noon. We left the site and headed for the mountains. Yigal reminded us that the Essenes in Qumran also lived in caves, sometimes carving them out of the hillside themselves.

"One of these caves," he said, "could certainly be called a library, because we found so many remnants of scrolls in it. It appears that the members of the sect came here to borrow scrolls they wanted to read, just like in a lending library today."

"Mom, I'm thirsty and I need to pee," whined Jonathan, my little brother.

"Really, Jonathan," said Yigal. "On the Sabbath! It's a good thing that you only need to pee. Do you know that the members of the Judean Desert sect were only allowed to pee on Saturdays and not do their other business? This was because of the holiness of the Sabbath, of course."

Mom and Dad laughed. Jonathan said, "It's lucky that I'm not a member, then," and went off to find a secluded place.

All around us we saw more pools carved into the rock.

"Where did all the water come from?" I asked.

"Partly from seasonal floods, and partly from the rainwater that was collected in the pools," Yigal explained. "There were also springs in the area, and the Essenes built channels from the springs to the pools. They needed a lot of water – for drinking, as it's so hot here, for washing, and for purifying. The members of the Judean Desert sect washed often and were extremely careful about cleanliness."

"This would have been a good place for those of us who hate taking showers!" said Mom, looking at me.

"No children were allowed here," Yigal said, "only boys who had reached maturity were accepted into the sect."

"So where did the wives and children live?" Dad wanted to know.

"According to sect rules, they were forbidden to enter the settlement. In the burial grounds we found 1,100 graves – mostly men, but at a little distance from them, a few graves of women and children. Maybe these were family members who came to visit men in the sect or asked especially to be buried near them."

"For a group of hermits in the desert they seem to have been very well organized," Dad remarked. "Who was in charge?"

"That's a hard question," Yigal answered. "The scrolls seem to show that they had a leader, whom they called 'Teacher of Righteousness,' but scholars cannot agree as to exactly who he was."

Yigal continued guiding us. But when we reached the parking lot, we suddenly realized that Jonathan was nowhere in sight.

Chapter 5 | Jonathan Makes an Amazing Discovery

That was the moment that broke the calm. My mother turned pale, probably imagining Jonathan lying at the foot of a cliff. My father and Yigal divided the area between them. Each one went in an opposite direction. I wanted to go with them, but Mom said: "Stay right here with me, and don't move!"

We heard Dad and Yigal yelling for Jonathan. But the only answer was the echo of their voices. Just as Mom was about to call the police on her cellular phone, we saw little Jonathan huffing and puffing as he climbed out of a ditch in the distance.

"Look what I've found," he shouted.

"Jonathan, are you crazy? Where have you been? Nobody walks around here alone!" – that was my Mom angry and relieved at the same time. Dad and Yigal came running. Jonathan was holding something in his hand. Yigal took it and began to brush off the dirt and sand. It turned out to be a sardine can, and we all burst out laughing.

"What's so funny?" asked Jonathan, looking offended.

"Jonathan, the Judean Desert sect didn't eat canned sardines 2,000 years ago," I explained.

My little brother looked embarassed.

"Where did you find this?" asked Yigal, who did not want Jonathan

to feel insulted.

Jonathan led us to a nearby ditch, and pointed to the bottom. "Way down there," he said.

"Where?" asked Yigal, turning pale. "In this ditch?"

"Yes, right down here."

Yigal sat down heavily and pulled off his sunglasses, sighing deeply.

"Yigal, what's the problem?" Dad asked, "it's only a sardine can."

"It's not just any sardine can. It's a disaster!" pronounced Yigal. "This is the ditch that we have been excavating. We were sure that we had already reached remains of the sect, and now because of Jonathan's find, it is clear that for the past week we have been digging the debris of previous archaeologists."

"Debris?" I asked.

"Yes, debris. That's what we call the earth you find when you dig. You remove it from the ditch so that you can go on digging. Those sardines were eaten by archaeologists over forty years ago," Yigal said, turning to my brother. "You have helped us a lot. Now we can stop wasting time and dig faster."

I was astonished to think that even a rusty old sardine can could be important to an archaeologist. I wished I had been the one to find it. We said goodbye to Yigal and promised to come again and check on the progress of the dig. Yigal stood near the ditch holding the "ancient" sardine can, thinking.

We drove to Ein Gedi. The midday sun was burning hot, and we could hardly wait to jump into the pool at Nahal David for a nice cool, relaxing swim.

Chapter 6 | I Tie Up Loose Ends

On Monday afternoon I went back to the Israel Museum. In a few days, I would have to hand in my report on the Dead Sea Scrolls, and I felt that I knew enough about the scrolls and the people who had written them. I had spoken to experts and I had been to the place where the scrolls were written. All I had to do now was see the objects themselves. Nobody had been murdered and nothing had been stolen, but I still felt sort of like a detective, or at least like a real scholar.

This time, as I walked up to the Shrine of the Book, it all seemed so clear! The black wall represented the Sons of Darkness and the white dome represented the Sons of Light. The way they faced each other, they seemed to be at war. Now I understood that the entrance was like the caves where the scrolls were found, and the darkness and chill inside were just like the conditions in the caves.

I said hello to my friend the guard, and went inside. On the way I passed the two big jars in which the scrolls had been found. Wait a moment! Of course, the lids of the jars were the same shape as the dome of the Shrine! So the dome was a kind of "lid" for the "jar" where the scrolls were kept. What a cool idea!

Now the scrolls were like old friends. I saw the War between the Sons of Light and the Sons of Darkness, the Community Rule, and other scrolls that were found in the desert such as the Temple Scroll, the Nahum Commentary, and the Book of Psalms. All these scrolls belonged to the Judean Desert sect and all were written or copied by them. In the heart of the dome, in a round glass case, higher than all the others, was the scroll of the Book of Isaiah.

This scroll is the most important one and therefore has a place of honor. The round showcase has a pillar at the center that looks like the wooden rods on which the Torah scroll is rolled in the synagogue. In Hebrew, these rods are called "trees of life."

The label next to the scroll said this was only a photograph of the scroll.

A school group stood nearby with a guide from the Museum. I recognized her as a guide from the Ruth Youth Wing who had taken our class on a tour of the Museum last year. The guide told the group that at first, the real scroll was on display in that showcase, but strong electric light shining on it all day made the scroll begin to crumble, so it was removed and put in a protected place. One

fragment of the real Isaiah scroll was displayed in a side showcase.

The guide also said that these scrolls were so important because they were a thousand years older than any biblical manuscript known to us, and they confirmed that 2,000 years ago the words in the text were almost exactly the same as in the Bible that we have today.

The guide pointed out the sheets of parchment and how they were joined together with needle and thread. She also said that all the books of the Bible had been found at Qumran, each written on a separate scroll, apart from the books of Nehemiah and Esther.

"Was there only one copy of each book?" asked one of the girls.

"No, some were found in several copies, like Deuteronomy, Psalms, and Isaiah, which were found in the most copies. There were fifteen Isaiah scrolls, but only one of them was complete," said the guide. "Scientists pieced together some of these scrolls like 1,000-piece jigsaw puzzles. The Bedouins understood that these were valuable things, and they searched every cave they could find. Sometimes they cut up scrolls, in order to sell them piece by piece. Putting them together was a very complicated business."

"What are those lines on the scrolls?" a boy asked.

"Before writing on them, the scribes used a sharp instrument to carve lines in the scrolls. The letters hung in straight lines from them, just like laundry on a clothesline, instead of the letters resting on the line, the way you are taught to write today. Sometimes a tattered scroll was mended with patches pasted on the sheepskin. If they wanted to make corrections, these were added above the line," continued the guide. "The Judean Desert sect wrote the scrolls in a square script, printed, in a

way that anyone can still read today. If you look closely, you will see that the name of God is written in a different, more ancient, Hebrew script because of its holiness."

Next to the display case containing the Temple Scroll, the most beautiful and the longest scroll (more than eight meters long), I saw two guards and two other people trying to open a case. One of them was my friend.

"What's going on?" I whispered.

"One of the instruments in the case is broken, and the laboratory people want to replace it. We're guarding them."

"What? You have to guard Museum workers?" I asked.

"Yes, that's the law," said the guard. "No-one's allowed to open the display cases or remove the scrolls without guards."

"What if the Israel Museum wants to send a scroll to another country to display in their museum?" I asked.

"That rarely happens, but when it does, it can only be with the approval of the Israeli government, because of the scrolls' tremendous importance to the Jewish people and the whole world."

Wow, I thought to myself. It all started with my teacher, Dorit, and ended up with the Israeli government.

Here was the perfect last sentence for my report.

And what did I get out of all this?

I handed in my assignment and got an A+. I met loads of interesting people. I got to see the oldest copies of the Bible in the whole world, and I discovered that every archaeologist is really a detective!

Captions

p. 15   A section of the Community Rule scroll

p. 28   Charred dates from Qumran

p. 29   Serving and eating utensils from Qumran

p. 31   Limestone cups from Qumran, apparently used for ritual hand washing (top)

p. 31   "Sundial" from Qumran (bottom)

p. 32   A section of the War Scroll

p. 43   Restored desks from Qumran

p. 59   Jars in which the Dead Sea Scrolls were hidden

Photo Credits